Tundra Books, an imprint of Penguin Random House Canada Young Readers,
a Penguin Random House Company

First published in Great Britain in 2019 by Andersen Press Ltd.

Published simultaneously in the United States of America by Tundra Books of Northern New York,
an imprint of Penguin Random House Canada Young Readers, a Penguin Random House Company

Library and Archives Canada Cataloguing in Publication available upon request

ISBN 978-0-7352-6715-2

Library of Congress Control Number: 2019936621

The artwork in this book is a collage of hand-painted textures and digital illustrations.
The text was set in Sassoon Infant.

Printed and bound in Canada

www.penguinrandomhouse.ca

2 3 4 5   24 23 22 21 20

Penguin
Random House
TUNDRA BOOKS

THE BUTT N BOOK

SALLY NICHOLLS

BETHAN WOOLLVIN

tundra

Here's a **red** button.
I wonder what happens
when you press it?

Here's an **orange** button.
What does the orange button do?

It's a clapping button!
Everybody clap!

What happens when you
press the **blue** button?

It's a **singing** button!

"The wheels on the bus go round and round..."

Does it know any other songs?

Shall we press
the **green** button now?

Thbbppppt!

Thbbpppt!

Excuse me, say sorry
at once.

I'm warning you.
This is your last chance.

Well, if you're going to be like that,
we're going to press the yellow button instead.

It's a **bouncing** button!
Everybody bounce!

Bounce!

Bounce!

Help!

Press the **pink** button or we'll be bouncing forever.

Hurray, it's
a **hug** button.

Hug time!

That's the best
button of all.

You **do** want to press the next button?

Are you sure?

Are you really sure?

Really, really, **really** sure?

All right then . . .

press the
purple
button.

Please, press the **pink** button, **quick!**

"Hey–
this is HUG
time!"

Ahh . . .
that's better.
Hug time.

Oh no, it's that rude **green** button again.
Have you learned any manners yet?

Back to the **red** button again.

Do you remember
what noise it makes?

Beep!

Look, it's a **new** button.

What does a **white** button do?

Shhhh . . . it's a **sleeping** button.

Goodnight, everyone.